A Note to Parents

DK READERS is a compelling program for beginning readers, designed in conjunction with leading literacy experts, including Dr. Linda Gambrell, Director of the Eugenge T. Moore School of Education at Clemson University. Dr. Gambrell has served on the Board of Directors of the International Reading Association and as President of the National Reading Conference.

Beautiful illustrations and superb full-color photographs combine with engaging, easy-to-read stories to offer a fresh approach to each subject in the series. Each DK READER is guaranteed to capture a child's interest while developing his or her reading skills, general knowledge, and love of reading.

The four levels of DK READERS are aimed at different reading abilities, enabling you to choose the books that are exactly right for your child:

Level 1 – Beginning to read
Level 2 – Beginning to read alone
Level 3 – Reading alone
Level 4 – Proficient readers

The "normal" age at which a child begins to read can be anywhere from three to eight years old, so these levels are intended only as a general guideline.

No matter which level you select, you can be sure that you are helping your child learn to read, then read to learn!

DK

LONDON, NEW YORK, DELHI,
MUNICH, AND MELBOURNE

Created by Leapfrog Press Ltd

Project Editor Dawn Sirett
Art Editor Miranda Kennedy

For Dorling Kindersley
Senior Editor Mary Atkinson
Managing Art Editor Peter Bailey
US Editor Regina Kahney
Production Melanie Dowland
Illustrator Tony Smith
History Consultant Anne Millard

Reading Consultant
Linda B. Gambrell, Ph.D.

First American Edition, 1999
03 04 05 06 07 10 9 8 7 6 5 4 3 2
Published in the United States by DK Publishing, Inc.
375 Hudson Street, New York, New York 10014

Published in Great Britain by Dorling Kindersley Limited.

Library of Congress Cataloging-in-Publication Data
Bull, Angela, 1936-
 Time traveler / by Angela Bull. -- 1st American ed.
  p. cm. -- (Dorling Kindersley readers. Level 3)
 Summary: Sophie and Jake, who don't find history interesting, test
a computer program that shows what life was like in ancient Rome,
Viking times, the Renaissance, the Gold Rush era, World War Two,
and into the space age.
 ISBN 0-7894-4763-0 (hardcover). -- ISBN 0-7894-4762-2 (pbk.)
 [1. World history Fiction. 2. Time travel Fiction.] I. Title.
II. Series.
PZ7.B9112 Ti 1999
[Fic]--dc21   99-25596
                                                      CIP

Color reproduction by Colourscan, Singapore
Printed and bound in China by L Rex Printing Co., Ltd.

The publisher would like to thank the following for their kind permission
to reproduce their photographs: Key: b=bottom, t=top, r=right
AKG (London) Ltd: 27t, 27b, 39; **Bridgeman Art Library:** 20; **C.M. Dixon:**
7b; **Dorling Kindersley Picture Library/British Museum:** 19t; /**London
Planetarium, Madame Tussauds:** 42; /**Musée du louvre:** 23br; /**National
Maritime Museum:** 16–17b; **NASA/Kennedy Space Center:** 45t; **Peter
Newark's Pictures:** 32b, 35b, 41; **Science Photo Library:** 45b, 46;
Topham Picturepoint: 37b.
Additional credits: Luciano Corbella, Eugene Fleury, Gerald Wood,
John Woodcock (additional illustrations); Ermine Street Guard (artefacts p8);
Piers Tilbury (jacket design); Peter Anderson, Paul Bricknell, Peter Chadwick,
Stephen Conlin, Andy Crawford, Geoff Dann, Michael Dunning, Christi
Graham, Alan Hills, Colin Keates, Dave King, Liz McAulay, Nick Nicholls,
Philippe Sebert, Karl Shone, James Stevenson, Matthew Ward, Jerry Young
(photography for DK); Liz Moore (picture research).
All other images © Dorling Kindersley
For further imformation see: www.dkimages.com

Discover more at
www.dk.com

Contents

TIME TRAVELER

CHILDREN THROUGH TIME

Written by Angela Bull

DK

DK Publishing, Inc.

Children through time

" 'As the game ended, the roar from the crowd was deafening. The Denver Broncos had set football history, winning their second Super Bowl in a row!' "

Mr. Johnson read Sophie's history homework.

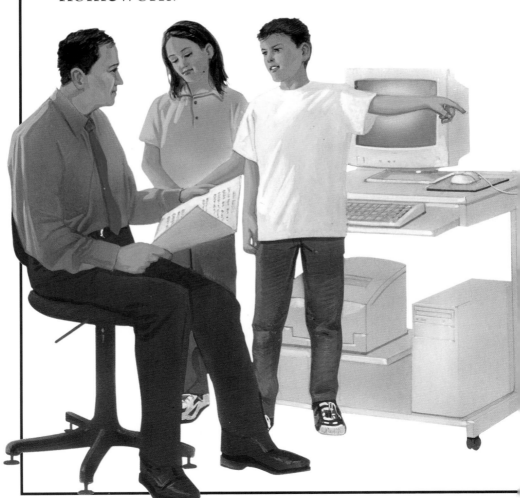

"What's this?" he asked. "I told you to write an essay about the most exciting event of the last 2,000 years. Sports didn't begin with the Super Bowl, you know.

"Now what about you, Jake?" Mr. Johnson turned to a boy next to Sophie. "Where's your essay?"

"History homework's boring," said Jake. "I went exploring with my brother on my new bike."

"Then you will have to do some extra studies at lunchtime," said Mr. Johnson. "Once you've eaten, you can both come back here and help me with something."

After lunch, instead of going out to play, Sophie and Jake went gloomily to Mr. Johnson's classroom. The last thing they wanted to do was more history!

Ancient Rome

Mr. Johnson switched on the class computer and put in a disk.

"A software company sent me a new CD-ROM called *Children Through Time*," he explained. "They want to know if it gets students interested in history. So you two are perfect to test it."

"This doesn't sound bad," said Jake.

"Not for history," added Sophie.

Colored letters unscrolled across the computer screen and spelled out WHIRLIGIG. Jake pressed "Enter." A funny little creature with bug eyes popped up. A voice came from the PC.

"I'm Whirligig. I spin circles of time, backwards, forwards, never stopping. Type in your favorite subject."

"Sports," Sophie typed in quickly.

Whirligig began to spin. Rings of numbers raced across the screen.

Whirligig

"They're dates!" said Jake, as the rings opened out and revealed a great city.

"Ancient Rome in the year AD 110," said Whirligig. "For 500 years it was the capital of one of the greatest empires the world has ever known."

Model of ancient Rome

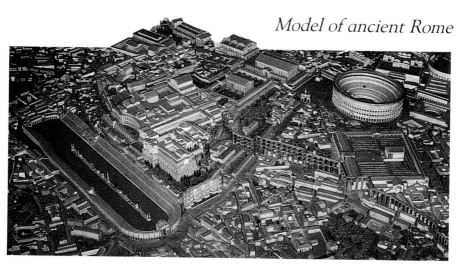

Circus Maximus, the racetrack (left), held chariot races.

"Powerful emperors ruled Rome," Whirligig went on. "With armies of expert soldiers, divided into legions, the emperors conquered lands from Britain to Egypt, including most of Europe. Everywhere they went, they built roads and cities, developed trade and industry ..."

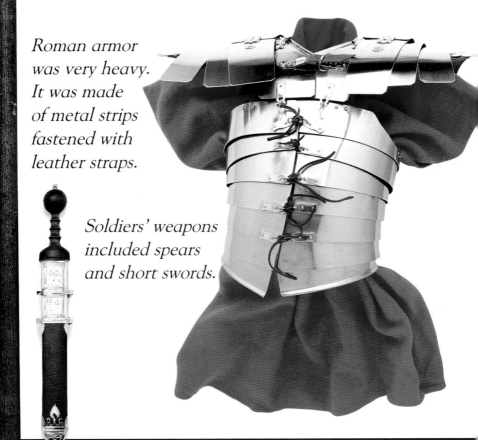

Roman armor was very heavy. It was made of metal strips fastened with leather straps.

Soldiers' weapons included spears and short swords.

Roman empire

Rome was built in 753 BC. By 275 BC, it ruled Italy and began to expand. By AD 117, Rome was at its height. It ruled all the lands in dark orange on this map.

"This isn't sports!" interrupted Sophie. She typed the word again.

"Throughout the empire," Whirligig continued, "people liked to watch sports in their spare time. Roman chariot races were among the most exciting sporting events in history. Click the video button to watch one."

"Here we go," said Sophie as she clicked the button.

The screen showed a close-up of a racetrack. Tiers of seats rose to the sky.

People took their places, eating pies and fruit. Two boys with blue banners chatted eagerly.

"Marcus needs one more win," said one of the boys. "With the money for his prize, he'll be able to buy his freedom."

A man with a white banner sneered.

"Slaves shouldn't be allowed to go free. Who'd do all the hard work?"

The boys tried to ignore him.

"Anyway, that young slave Marcus won't beat Gaius," the man went on. "Gaius is the best and he's in the Whites – the emperor's favorite team."

"If Marcus takes the inside track, he'll pass Gaius," the boy insisted.

Sophie began to laugh.

"It's like any sport!" she exclaimed. "Fans talking team tactics and eating. I'm going to support the Blues."

Suddenly, two chariots charged onto the track, their charioteers grasping the horses' reins. Marcus wore blue. Gaius wore white.

The starter dropped a white cloth. The horses dashed around the track. Marcus fought to take the inside lane, but Gaius steered too tightly. Marcus had to pull back.

"He's lost!" Sophie wailed.

Thinking the same, Gaius slackened his speed. That was Marcus's chance. He stormed past on the outside and won the race.

Sophie cheered. Blues' fans yelled.

The old city of Rome flicked back onto the screen.

"Why aren't there chariot races in Rome any more?" Sophie wondered.

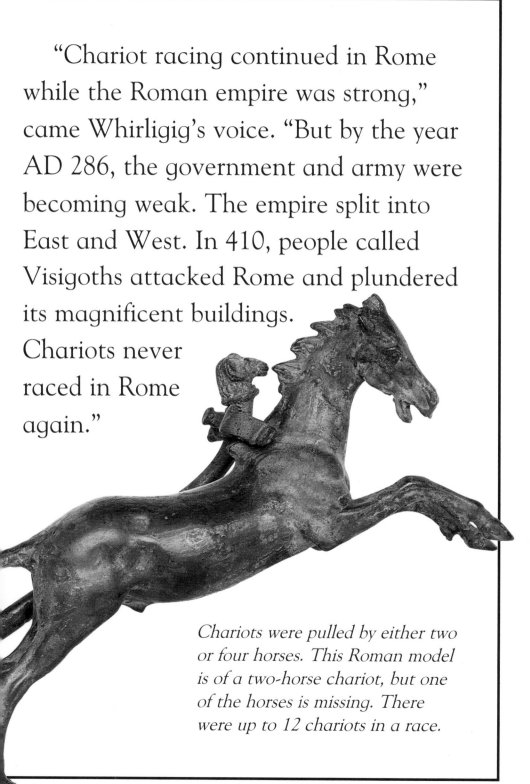

"Chariot racing continued in Rome while the Roman empire was strong," came Whirligig's voice. "But by the year AD 286, the government and army were becoming weak. The empire split into East and West. In 410, people called Visigoths attacked Rome and plundered its magnificent buildings. Chariots never raced in Rome again."

Chariots were pulled by either two or four horses. This Roman model is of a two-horse chariot, but one of the horses is missing. There were up to 12 chariots in a race.

Viking explorers

"My turn now," said Jake. Thinking of his new bike, he typed in "Exploring."

Rome faded away and in Whirligig's spinning rings the years rushed forward. Darkness closed in. Through it a wooden boat loomed onto the screen, approaching a bleak headland at sunset. Whirligig began his explanation.

"This is Norway in the year AD 1000. A Viking longboat is returning home. The Vikings were the finest shipbuilders of their time. They sailed from their Scandinavian homelands as far east as Russia and as far west as North America. They were great explorers, raiders, and traders."

"I wonder who's on the boat," murmured Jake, "and where they've been. Let's find out."

He clicked the video button.

As the longboat approached against the sun, people emerged from nearby wooden huts. A young boy gazed out from the headland.

"Bjorn!" a woman shouted to him. "It's Seabird – your brother Sven's ship."

The longboat's sail billowed as its dragon prow grated on the beach. People ran forward to haul the boat in.

Soon strong warriors were unloading heavy wooden chests filled with gold and silver.

"We got to England!" a crewman shouted. "What a country. Wealthy and fertile. One raid and we're rich!"

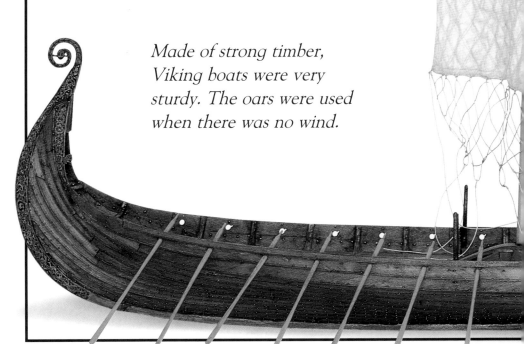

Made of strong timber, Viking boats were very sturdy. The oars were used when there was no wind.

Viking warriors

Viking warriors raided across Europe, looking for land and treasure. They wore chain mail or leather tunics. Their swords and battle axes were made of iron and wood.

Dragon figurehead for prow of ship

A carved figurehead was often attached to the prow, or front end, of a Viking ship.

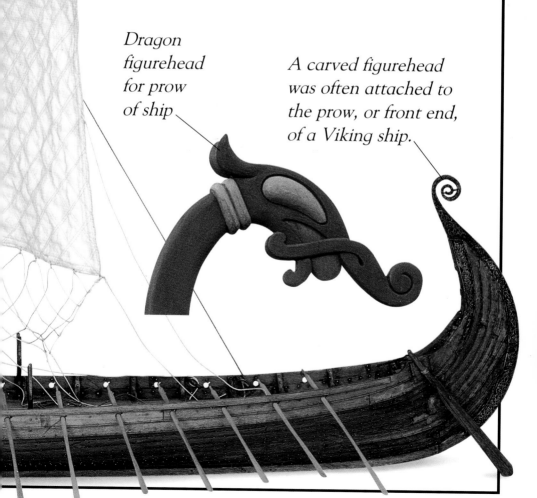

"Who's he?"
wondered Jake,
watching a tall
warrior approach.

Bjorn, the boy
from the headland,
rushed up to
the warrior.

"Well done, Sven!"
Sven walked past without replying.
"What's wrong?" Bjorn asked.
"You've changed. Were you wounded?"

"No," Sven answered. "But I heard
something and I didn't want to come
home. We met some other warriors,
who told wonderful stories. They'd been
to Greenland with Chief Eric the Red.
They're sure there's a land farther west,
with great mountains and forests."

"Is there a land beyond Greenland?" demanded Bjorn, surprised.

Sven nodded.

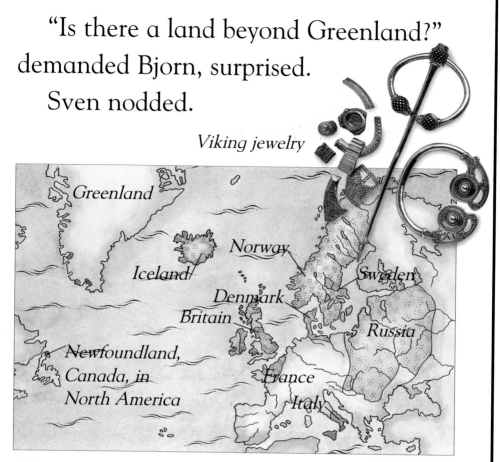

Viking jewelry

Greenland

Norway

Iceland

Sweden

Denmark

Britain

Russia

Newfoundland, Canada, in North America

France

Italy

Vikings raided, traded, or settled in the brown areas.

"No one has been there. These warriors caught sight of it, but the wind was too strong for them to land. Next year, Eric's son, Leif the Lucky, is organizing an expedition to sail there. I want to go with him. I will! I must!"

This modern tapestry shows Leif spotting North America.

The video ended. Whirligig popped up on the screen again.

"Test your knowledge!" he cried. "Which land did Leif the Lucky go on to discover? China, Australia, or North America?"

"I don't remember Whirligig saying the Vikings reached China or Australia," said Sophie.

"No. Let's type in North America," said Jake.

"Correct!" said Whirligig. "Leif the Lucky and his crew were the first Europeans to reach North America. Historians think that they landed in Canada around the year 1001. Some Vikings even settled there for a while."

"Vikings were better explorers than me and my brother," said Jake. "Imagine sailing off and finding a new continent!"

"People can fly to other continents now," said Sophie. "I have an idea!"

She typed in "Flying."

Whirligig began to spin. The rings whirled out again, faster and faster.

The Renaissance

Green light blazed from the middle of the whirling rings.

Emerald

"Is that an emerald?" Jake wondered.

A richly dressed man appeared on the screen. He hung an emerald necklace around a young girl's neck.

"That's Giovanni and his daughter Isabella," said Whirligig. "They're in Florence, Italy, in 1500. It's the time called the Renaissance*, or 'rebirth.' For centuries the Church had taught that life on earth was only a preparation for heaven. Renaissance scholars developed new ways of thinking. They took ideas from ancient Greece and Rome ..."

"Can't we skip this?" grumbled Jake.

*Pronounced REN-uh-sonse

"No. Rome had chariot races. I liked it," said Sophie. "Let's keep watching."

"Human life gained new value," said Whirligig. "Artists drew human bodies more accurately. Merchants bought art and rich jewels to show their importance."

"I didn't know art had anything to do with history," said Jake. "I like art."

He clicked the video button.

Mona Lisa by Leonardo da Vinci

Many fine buildings and paintings were produced during the Renaissance.

St. Peter's in Rome

A jeweler bowed and produced a mirror. Isabella stared at her reflection.

"In the convent I had to wear gray," she murmured.

"Times change," answered Giovanni. "Your education with the nuns is over. You're fourteen and ready for marriage. You need fine clothes and jewels."

He handed a purse to the jeweler.

"It's perfect. Good work," he said.

The old jeweler sighed. Once he'd made holy things to adorn churches. Now merchants like Giovanni demanded to be more splendid than God.

Isabella and Giovanni went out into the street. With a shout, men leaped from a dark alley, brandishing daggers.

Giovanni's servants drew their swords. Isabella dived through a small door.

The door led into a studio where an artist was studying some sketches.

"Help!" Isabella shrieked. "My father's being attacked!"

"Quick! Come inside. You'll be safe here," the artist reassured her. "Florence swarms with thieves on the lookout for rich targets. Let's see what's happening."

He peered out a window.

"It's all right. Your father is safe inside a church and his men are winning."

"Good!" whispered Isabella.

She looked so terrified that the artist held out the sketches to distract her. They showed people fastened to frames that looked like birds' wings.

"What are these?" Isabella asked.

"Drawings by Leonardo da Vinci," the artist replied. "He's a brilliant painter and inventor. He believes people can learn to fly like birds."

"See if you can fly. Flap your arms up and down," Sophie told Jake, laughing.

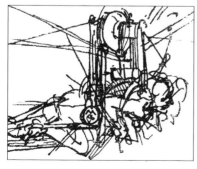

Leonardo da Vinci's flying machine sketch

While Jake flapped, she clicked on the sketches for more information.

"These designs were probably the first scientific attempt to invent a flying machine," came Whirligig's voice. "Leonardo made them 400 years before airplanes were invented. The designs were discovered centuries after he died."

"Wow!" exclaimed Jake. "Imagine drawing something people will look at hundreds of years later. I'm going to write my history essay about Leonardo and draw pictures of his inventions."

"Good idea," said Sophie as she clicked the button to continue the video.

"Do you think people will ever learn to fly?" Isabella asked the artist.

"We're learning more, traveling farther," he replied. "We print books, make clocks. Anything's possible."

A servant opened the door.

"All's safe, Miss Isabella."

"I'd be safer if I could fly away."

As Isabella spoke, the flying machine seemed to float off the table, spinning away into Whirligig's rings.

Leonardo's flying machine would not have flown, but it's an amazing early attempt at flying. This is a modern reconstruction of the machine.

Gold rush

"I liked Isabella's necklace," said Sophie.

"But clothes aren't part of history," scoffed Jake. "Not like art."

"I bet they are," Sophie argued. "Let's find out. I know." She typed in "Jeans."

Whirligig's spinning rings turned into wheels, traveling across mountains and prairies in sun, rain, and snow.

"1850 in California. Gold was found here in 1848," said Whirligig. "By 1849, thousands of people were rushing across the United States in wagons to search for gold. You'll see two orphans, Ellen and Clem, arriving at a mining town."

"Sounds great!" exclaimed Jake, clicking the video button.

A wagon appeared on the screen.

A girl and a boy were huddled in the wagon, staring at a shabby town ahead.

"It's horrible," wailed Ellen. "Let's go back. I don't care about getting rich."

"We have to try," answered Clem. He drove on.

A filthy, unshaven man grinned at the two children.

"Welcome to Miseryville."

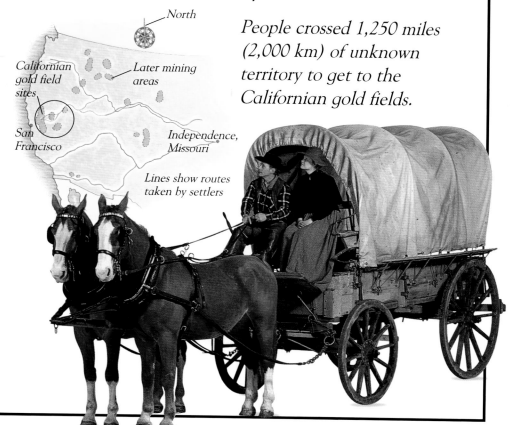

North

Californian gold field sites

Later mining areas

San Francisco

Independence, Missouri

Lines show routes taken by settlers

People crossed 1,250 miles (2,000 km) of unknown territory to get to the Californian gold fields.

Clem started to search for gold the next day. The river was crowded with prospectors, all searching too. They elbowed him away. Finally he found

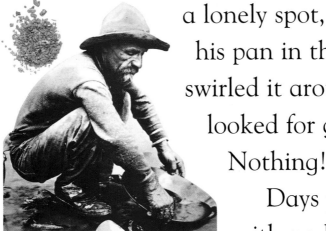

a lonely spot, dipped his pan in the water, swirled it around, and looked for gold. Nothing!

Days passed with no luck. Ellen despaired. And she was so cold!

Any gold sank to the bottom of the prospectors' pans.

A prospector's wife stopped by the wagon to offer some help.

"You need pants to keep warm," she said. "I'll get you some work pants like the ones the prospectors wear."

"Pants!" Ellen looked horrified.

"What's wrong with pants?" wondered Jake, staring at the screen.

"I think only men wore them then," said Sophie. "If they were work pants, I bet they were jeans."

Tough pants

Jeans are made of denim – a hard-wearing fabric. American workmen wore denim pants in the 1850s. Levi Strauss first sold jeans with rivets holding the seams in 1873.

The prospector's wife
brought Ellen some jeans.
Reluctantly, Ellen pulled
them on. They were rough,
but so warm! Suddenly,
she felt better. With cornmeal and eggs,
she began cooking pancakes for Clem.

A passing prospector sniffed.

"That smells good. I'll trade you
a pinch of gold dust for a pancake!"

Soon other men gathered around.

"You cooking for everyone, Miss?"

Ellen tossed more and more pancakes.
When Clem got back, she'd had an idea.

"Forget the river," she said.
"We'll make our fortune this way."

She tossed another pancake.
It flipped, spun …

Whirligig popped up again.

"California boomed!" he announced. "By 1849, the population had risen from 20,000 to more than 100,000 and it went on growing. Many of those who didn't get rich stayed on, and salesmen, traders, and farmers joined them. Towns, roads, and railways were built ..."

"Okay," Jake interrupted. "I'm hungry after seeing those pancakes."

He typed "Chocolate."

A thriving gold-mining town

World War Two

Whirligig's rings circled and swirled. Airplanes dived through them. Bombs exploded and guns roared.

"In 1933," said Whirligig, "Adolf Hitler came to power in Germany. He wanted to expand German territory. In 1939, Germany invaded Poland, so Britain and France declared war on Germany. By 1940, Hitler had conquered much of mainland Europe and tried to bomb Britain into surrendering. In 1941, America entered the war and American troops came to Britain to join the war effort. Watch the video to see David's birthday party and one way American troops helped British people."

"Party!" Sophie exclaimed eagerly. She clicked the video button.

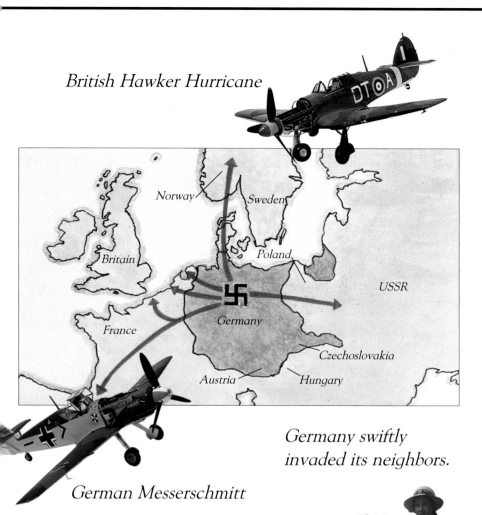

British Hawker Hurricane

Norway
Sweden
Britain
Poland
USSR
France
Germany
Czechoslovakia
Austria
Hungary

German Messerschmitt

Germany swiftly invaded its neighbors.

British evacuees

Children were evacuated, or sent away, from cities to the country, where they would be safe from the bombing. But thousands became lonely and returned home.

A small boy and his mother were standing at a table. The boy looked very miserable.

"No party, Mom! It doesn't feel like my birthday at all."

"You know food is rationed – clothes, too," said Mom. "We don't get much in exchange for coupons in our ration books. I've done the best I can."

There was bread with meat paste and a cake without icing or candles. David and his mom wore old, patched clothes. Just then an older girl came in.

"Susan!" David shouted. "Have you got my present?"

Susan gave him a plain brown pencil. There was no wrapping paper or card.

David stamped angrily.

"I wanted a train! You had good presents when you were nine. I haven't even had any chocolate."

"There's a war on!" cried Mom.

Angry and upset, Susan ran out of the house. She collided with a soldier.

"Hey! What's up?" the soldier asked.

"Everything!" cried Susan. "It's my brother's birthday. There are no toys or candy. We can't have a party with rationed food. Dad's away fighting ..."

"Maybe I can help," said the soldier.

"You're American!" gasped Susan.

"Sure. I'm Clark. Give me half an hour. I'll get some things from my base."

Soon Clark was back unloading packages – cans of ham and fruit, butter, chewing gum, stockings for Mom – unbelievable in wartime England.

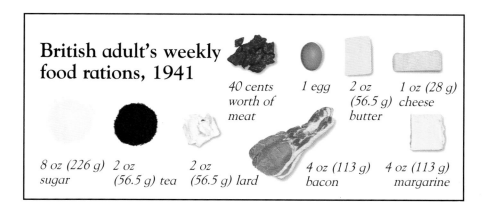

British adult's weekly food rations, 1941

40 cents worth of meat

1 egg

2 oz (56.5 g) butter

1 oz (28 g) cheese

8 oz (226 g) sugar

2 oz (56.5 g) tea

2 oz (56.5 g) lard

4 oz (113 g) bacon

4 oz (113 g) margarine

"And here's the birthday present," said Clark.

He handed David a box filled with chocolate.

David passed the box around the table, around and around, spinning in a ring.

American troops made friends with British people.

Whirligig appeared with more information.

"In 1944, British and American troops recaptured France. Russian troops were moving towards the German capital. In May 1945, Germany surrendered. But life in Britain took some time to get back to normal. Rationing lasted until 1954!"

Space age

"That war was awful," sighed Sophie.

"Let's try a topic where countries are now helping each other, not fighting," said Jake. He typed "Space exploration."

Whirligig's rings blazed and dazzled. Rockets blasted off all over the screen.

"First space traveler, 1961," announced Whirligig. "First person on the moon, 1969. Space probes to Venus, Jupiter, Saturn, Mars …"

Space probes

Probes are unmanned spacecraft. They carry cameras and other equipment for exploring space, and send data back to Earth. The Galileo probe took off in 1989 to explore Jupiter.

Galileo probe

"Hang on!" exclaimed Jake.

He clicked "Video."

The rockets faded. An ordinary classroom appeared on the screen.

"That's odd," said Sophie, puzzled.

"The United States, 1996. Meet Joe. He's going to be linked with Saturn," explained Whirligig.

"How?" Sophie demanded.

She stared at a boy who sat alone, looking angry. A girl came up.

"What's wrong, Joe?" she asked.

"Haven't you heard?" said Joe. "My sister Anna's starring in the school ballet. She goes on and on about it. 'I'm a star! I'm a star!' It's all I hear."

"Why don't you send yourself to another planet," said the girl, laughing.

"What d'you mean, Kate?" Joe asked.

"It's on a website," explained Kate. "The Cassini space probe is going to carry people's names to Saturn. You can send in your signature and it'll be carried through space on a special disk."

"Can anyone do it?" asked Joe.

"Yes. I'm going to. People are even sending their dog's paw prints!"

"So a living creature on Saturn might see my name?" marveled Joe.

"That's right – after Cassini reaches Saturn in 2004," replied Kate.

"Maybe one day I'll go to Saturn and find my name," said Joe. He closed his eyes. "It makes my head spin."

The screen suddenly flicked to Cape Canaveral, Florida. A huge launch rocket carried the Cassini space probe.

Launch of Cassini

"It's October the 15th, 1997," said Whirligig. "Cassini is about to be launched. Two, one, zero. Blast off!"

A giant explosion rocketed Cassini into space. It soared high and was soon just a tiny pinprick of light.

Whirligig popped back on the screen.

"Space!" he cried. "The future!"

"Yes," said Jake to Sophie. "I bet there'll be loads of history happening out there in space in the new millennium."

Cassini space probe

An artist's impression of Cassini releasing a smaller space probe over Titan, Saturn's largest moon, in 2004

"And lots on Earth, too," said Sophie.

Mr. Johnson came over and switched off the computer. They'd forgotten he was in the room.

"What d'you think of history now?" he asked.

"It's exciting," answered Jake. "All that exploring in faraway places."

"But it's near to us, too," added Sophie. "Sports, wearing jewelry or jeans, going to birthday parties – people long ago weren't that different from us. I think that means the future won't be too different either."

"No, not too different," agreed Jake, "but just as exciting. We might be real explorers and travel to another planet."

"I'd still watch the Super Bowl, though," laughed Sophie.

Glossary and key people

Ancient Greece
A period in history beginning in about 2000 BC with the first great Greek civilization and lasting until Greece was conquered by Rome in 146 BC.

BC and AD
BC stands for "Before Christ." BC years are before Jesus's birth. AD stands for "Anno Domini," meaning "In the year of our Lord." AD years are after Jesus was born.

Chariot races
Races for horse-drawn carts that were first used in battles.

Charioteers
Chariot drivers – they were mostly slaves.

The Church
People following the Christian religion.

Circus Maximus
The great racetrack for chariot races in Rome, with room for 250,000 people.

Emperor
An empire's leader.

Empire
A group of countries ruled by one power.

Eric the Red
A Viking leader who explored Greenland in AD 984 and 985 and settled there.

Hitler, Adolf
Born in 1889, Hitler came to power in Germany in 1933 and tried to build an empire. He ruled until he died in 1945.

Legions
Divisions of Rome's army. Each one had about 5,000 soldiers.

Leif the Lucky
A Viking leader, son of Chief Eric the Red, and the first European to set foot in North America, around AD 1001.

Leonardo da Vinci
A great artist and inventor who lived from 1452 to 1519.

Longboat
A Viking warship.

Merchants
Business people who traded goods.

Prospectors
People who searched for gold.

Raiders
People who swiftly attacked towns and villages, taking treasure and slaves.

Ration
A fixed amount of certain foods and other items issued to each person during wartime.

Slaves
People who are owned by others. You could be born a slave or captured and made a slave.

Strauss, Levi
A manufacturer who lived from 1829 to 1902. He was the first person to sell riveted jeans, in 1873.

Traders
People who traded goods, such as ivory or furs, in exchange for other goods.

Visigoths
A German tribe.

Warriors
Fighters for a tribe.